Figure out How to Have Beautiful Skin Naturally

Let's be honest. I can't help thinking that insufficient individuals appear to need to set aside the effort to figure out how to have lovely skin normally. They would prefer essentially depend on the items that the significant beautifiers organizations continue siphoning out quite a long time after year. These items anyway are doing literally nothing at all in the method of helping individuals who need to have sound skin.

Truly the items that these large organizations put out joined by their million dollar advertisement crusades aren't even bravo. They contain fundamentally substance specialists as fixings that can have some intense impacts on the individual that routinely utilizes the items that contain them. A great many people have no clue exactly how genuine these impacts can end up being.

The significant makeup organizations would do nearly anything to keep shoppers from finding how to have wonderful skin normally, in light of the fact that that would imply that they would need to change to utilizing common fixings in their items so as to fulfill their now increasingly specific clients. Characteristic fixings cost more to process so the beauty care products industry all things considered wouldn't like to need to do this switch.

What they would prefer to do is have the option to keep on filling their items with synthetics and synthetic substances, on the grounds that these fixings don't require a lot of preparing. They are minimal effort, promptly accessible in huge amounts, and if you somehow happened to accept the gulp that the makers attempt to sell you they are alright for you to utilize. Nothing my companions could be further from reality.

I accept that everybody ought to teach themselves regarding the matter of how to have excellent skin normally, in light of the fact that then they would have the information to comprehend what fixings were beneficial for them, and which ones they ought to maintain a strategic distance from. The compound contaminants routinely utilized in items by the significant beautifiers organizations should be maintained a strategic distance from except if you need to harm your wellbeing.

These synthetic specialists have been demonstrated throughout the years to be endocrine framework disruptors, organ and neurotoxins, and are known to cause malignant growth. These fixings are just despite everything permitted to be utilized in the United States since guideline by the FDA to boycott their utilization was toppled in government court. The European Union was fruitful in having these fixings pulled from beautifying agents items.

In the event that you need to find out about how to have excellent skin normally you should take an exercise from a beauty care products organization in New Zealand that utilizes what are conceivably the best blends of characteristic fixings that the business has ever observed. Their items offer you regular fixings that securely and significantly increment the measure of collagen, elastin, and hyaluronic corrosive that your skin has I'm certain you know the well established saying, 'magnificence is quite shallow' and in one sense it is quite shallow in the event that you see the top layer, the main look see, a brief look at the external or the early introduction of what you at first observe from a position of self image, fantasy and being moderately sleeping to truth. Then again, excellence is straightforward, glowing sparkling essentialness and is other common when you see it from a position of profound truth as it communicates through twinkling eyes, delicate sound skin and gleaming hair that all offer the mystery of genuine magnificence - that which can't be moved by any cream, surgical tool or shivering consuming bothersome treatment that all guarantee unending young excellence. Magnificence is a mentality, a certainty, an internal knowing about insider facts for ageless and ever-enduring living, with elegance and gratefulness as our dearest sidekicks. Effortlessness and gratefulness for each human experience we have from youth, through the developing agonies of youthfulness ~ to the opportunity and investigation of our twenties - to the decisions of family, vocation and the horde of duties that spot our thirties, forties and onwards to the opportunity indeed of relinquishing all that we thought we were and reexamining ourselves so the times of the fifties, sixties and past can permit insight and youth blamelessness one again to play together and light the path for the ones coming up behind. I've found three little privileged insights for genuine glowing magnificence and I'm eager to impart them to you!

The Main Mystery does not shock anyone I'm certain, yet can be hard to regard and resolve to make a long lasting propensity.

It's essentially getting a decent night's rest, after quite a while after night, after a seemingly endless amount of time after month, after a seemingly endless amount of time after year for an amazing span. Obviously they'll be evenings were you lay alert pondering, stressing, plotting, arranging, wishing and abiding the hours as your hormones show signs of improvement of you, so I'm alluding to most of evenings for a mind-blowing duration. Focusing on it in your life of setting the stage, the room, the everyday practice and the environment to guarantee a decent night's rest since you're aware of everything about the mystery advantages of ongoing profoundly remedial, regenerative and reviving evening time rest. Any place you are and anyway you live, explorer or one who is settled down, you can decide to focus on it for your life of excellence. Along these lines, you get incalculable advantages both within and thus pervading through the outside of your body to communicate outwardly. These are the valuable extremely valuable hours whenever the entire body gets an opportunity to fix itself and fabricate over again for you. At the point when you are in the steady condition called home, it's far simpler than when you are voyaging.

It just takes a touch of arranging however, and this is what you do in each one of those occasions that you're in others' homes, lodgings, inns, on planes, trains, or anyplace else life takes you. You have little sacrosanct soothing assistants, similar to a comfortable cashmere shawl, an eye cushion and earplugs, a little scented flame, a global time piece to control your body, a lethargic time tea pack, your eco well disposed re-usable jug of water loaded up with your preferred water, and Evian fog for invigorating and hydrating the skin after waking.

In our general public in these difficult occasions it is said we normal however a couple of long stretches of profound rest every night, which is the reason so much publicizing centers around tranquilizers of different types; and on the repercussions of absence of rest, as diminished work time because of different issue of the psyche and body; inconsiderateness and weariness late morning, hyper sharpness at an inappropriate time of day, state of mind swings from overabundance caffeine utilization through a bunch of caffeinated drinks in addition to old fashioned mug of espresso or ten that are flushed for the duration of the day just to remain wakeful. Suppose you woke up toward the beginning of the day upbeat, revived and extended, yawned and tenderly along these lines invited your self to your day. Suppose you had the vitality to wake up only twenty minutes sooner than you used to in light of the fact that now following two or three months of consistent rest you need to practice before you even head for the primary cup of warm java! Goodness, and you're truly getting a charge out of that initially warm glass of water after waking to move your insides and to set the digestion murmuring for the remainder of the day. Indeed, old fashioned - molded rest. A basic choice, for example, not viewing the news an hour prior to sleep time for a month; or taking part in any warmed conversations with your mate, or protracted listening long distance races with lady friends does ponders for your brain and body in anticipation of rest. Doing nothing other than washing in the warm case of fragrant healing waters, engaging in sexual relations or looking delicately at inspiring otherworldly readings permits the psyche to quiet, unwind and let go. This will demonstrate the kindest most brilliant thing you can accomplish for your showing up and feeling excellent that I guarantee as long as you can remember will take on new viewpoints on the off chance that you can truly respect this significantly significant antiquated mystery.

Mystery Number Two is to see food as your medication and medication as your food. I know, here we go again with an old proven reality to accomplishing a lifetime of gleaming skin, well working organs, controlled smooth moving insides, and a feeling of quiet and clearness for the psyche that must be felt with customary interims of supplement thick nourishments on a predictable premise for quite a while, after a seemingly endless amount of time after month and a seemingly endless amount of time after year. I wager you were expecting some fresh out of the plastic new mystery at no other time knew about and I'm here to disclose to you that Grandmother knew something.

My Grandmother was excellent until the day she passed on and her skin was clear, her eyes shone with a flicker of youth and she was completely occupied with life every last bit of her 97 years of life! Her wellbeing was great, no diabetes, malignant growth, joint inflammation or heart issues and when I was a model in Toronto helping pay my way through school where she'd go to a style show at that point we'd go out with my companions a short time later, she'd drive - putting the pedal to the metal as is commonly said, snickering and hitting her knee with merriment since she simply adored being with we youngsters! She rested soundly due to a standard she kept all through as long as she can remember. She ate near the earth occasional nourishments, being mindful so as not to eat cold food sources in winter nor sweltering nourishments in summer; she tasted on a touch of fine liquor each other day before bed with her tea, and I do mean a pinch, a dazzling shot glass she was given in Paris, and it was a decent little one dissimilar to the enormous long 6 oz adaptations of today!

Here's the mystery of this mystery. It's in your view of, and commitment to this antiquated truth that will get you the outcomes you're searching for with the kicker being fast outcomes you'll really observe inside a month of legitimate eating! No more enlarged, rounded out look or feeling since you won't be aggravated within; not any more starving minutes where you could eat insatiably on the grounds that you let your self get too vacant and afterward you're excessively full and the psyche trips follow, and extremely, not any more arduous counter gainful hours at the exercise center where I have observed such a significant number of individuals sit in front of the television while they're working out that I can't envision why they aren't getting results they want ~ evident to me is the distinction between the body and the brain. The two of them should be ready when you pick, ingest, absorb, process and take out nourishments, and the two of them should be ready together while moving the body cheerfully to a conditioned, tight and sound look simply ideal for you. So how about we return to utilizing food as your medication and medication as your food. Consider it. It bodes well to have the possibility that in the event that you see everything that goes into your mouth as assisting with keeping you solid, delightful and ready to do, go, be and have anything you desire since you are brimming with vitality, you can check such a significant number of things off your can list! You won't really think about sick wellbeing since you're dealing with precisely what's in your control - that is, the thing that goes into your mouth! As you're fixation and center is after increasing the portion of feeling and looking better a seemingly endless amount of time after year, consistently, and it's good times! I nearly disregard ailment or absence of simplicity inside the body (which is the way I like to allude to sickness) until I get those month to month issues or feel an itch in my throat since I'm singing with other people who are very brimming with this season's cold virus. During these occasions, I quick and drink recuperating teas that my family has delighted in until the end of time! Teas are great wellbeing elevating endowments to give yourself, and we even do tea services with a cool minimal Japanese tea set we enjoyed,

You're companions with your body and your psyche and you'll be compensated for this. Here's a simple solution for your eating. Regardless of what you eat, consistently ask your self, 'where's the products of the soil the veggies'.! In any event, when I eat cereal in the first part of the day, including my ground flax seeds, a couple of various types of nuts, a couple of dried cranberries for pleasantness and a smidgen of delightful dim Vermont maple syrup, I toss in a couple of child carrots, a cut up bit of celery or cucumber and include a little bunch of my preferred natural product which is blueberries. Sounds strange to include the carrots and celery, yet know

Bliss, harmony, agreement, excellence, and marvel all originate from Nature with Affection. Nature additionally brings us uplifting news from reestablishment and recuperation. We are more joyful when we enjoy these positive encounters of nature. Furthermore, when we comprehend and acknowledge nature, we can likewise spare the earth.

Bliss and Nature

Nature and bliss have been connected since the beginning of time. At the point when we are cheerful we feel radiant. We go for the stars when we follow our fantasies. We climb mountains to arrive at our objectives. At the point when we relish the experience of Nature, we are more joyful.

The connection among joy and the harmony and congruity of nature is solid to such an extent, that when satisfaction scientists need to incite bliss for an analysis, they do as such by indicating pictures of nature or creatures playing.

You can test the connection yourself. Rate your present degree of joy on a size of 1 to 10 and compose it on a piece of paper. Overlay up the paper, and put in almost no time pondering your preferred involvement with nature. Recall the sentiment of the air on your skin, the scents and the sounds, just as what you saw.

setting it up on a sweet bamboo placemat, a red bloom fragrance based treatment flame and simple discussion. Odds are that if all that you eat is viewed as therapeutic including tastes of your preferred desserts, salty or smooth things, you'll keep up ideal wellbeing and excellence an amazing entirety.

Obviously we can't control many upsetting potential scenes of sick wellbeing that please because of hereditary qualities, or mishaps, or something like that, so please comprehend I'm alluding to our ability to pick flawless wellbeing that is our claim and that is inside our control.

On the off chance that your brain is quiet and you have the correct mentality around food, you can have a smidgen of everything without exception you love and it'll be acclimatized, processed and killed effectively in light of the fact that you're not going crazy about it's calories, fat, starch levels etcetera.

At the point when you are done, rate your joy again and compose the number outwardly of the paper-then think about. This equivalent examination has likewise been utilized to diminish pulses, circulatory strain and increment course.

From Nature With Affection?

Much the same as people, Nature likewise has its ruinous side. Yet, in the course of recent years, our thankfulness and comprehension of this side of nature that has helped us shield ourselves better from these ruinous powers. Albeit cataclysmic events despite everything happen, when we foresee them and make defensive move, the effect on human life drops significantly. Presently we realize that our activities can likewise crush nature. For instance, researchers have indicated that an unnatural weather change is expanding the number and seriousness of tropical storms. Our thankfulness, comprehension, and activity in agreement with nature can secure the earth and improve our lives on it.

Satisfaction and Critical thinking

As indicated by positive clinician Dr. Martin Seligman, our positive emotions have a developmental reason. Similarly as our negative sentiments dread and outrage set off our battle or flight real frameworks, our positive feelings joy and love-set off our structure and adjusting substantially frameworks. The more joyful we are, the more innovative we are and the better we are at taking care of issues that require thinking in new and various examples.
In the event that we are to on the whole comprehend the issues of contamination and a worldwide temperature alteration, or even world harmony and manageable economies, we will require only this sort of inventive reasoning. There is another connection among satisfaction and critical thinking in the law of fascination. What we acknowledge, increases in value. At the point when we set aside the effort to appreciate something and feel appreciation for it, its worth increments in our eyes and we pull in a greater amount of that esteem into our lives.

By valuing the earth and the worth that nature has for us, we pull in more nature and more answers for safeguard and secure nature in an amicable manner

Have you at any point gone for a stroll in the forested areas and felt a profound feeling of harmony and magnificence wrap you? Have you at any point strolled by the sea and detected the force and greatness of its excellence filling you with motivation? Have you at any point climbed a mountain and when you arrived at the top felt wonder as the broad vista before you blew your mind? Nature is an incredible asset for re-associating with your magnificence. The idea of your inclination in nature becomes animated as life blossoms normally around you. We are creatures of nature; it is our common state to cooperative with the components, to consider ourselves to be a piece of the entire and at one with all that is. Lining up with the magnificence of nature is adjusting to your own inclination, your feeling of prosperity and regular excellence too

At the point when we move our bodies, and our bodies are made for development, we permit energizing feel great synthetic concoctions to course all through our bodies. Endorphine's are our bodies characteristic antidepressants, they are invigorated by development and positive feelings, they get you and help up your state of mind as you get your internal motors consuming. Actuating endorphins through physical development as well as positive feelings and contemplations, can move your weight of despondency in a matter of moments by any means.

The stunning thing about the Beauty Walk as a methods for fending off melancholy is this; in addition to the fact that you are discharging the vibe great synthetic substances in your body, you are likewise implanting your Self with the excellence and radiance of life around you.

The Beauty Walk

The Beauty Walk is actually what you envision it to be, it is strolling and moving and taking in the abundance of life that encompasses you. Getting one with everything. For reality of each individual and each molecule on this planet is that we are completely made of a similar rich brilliant substance of the Universe. All that is of excellence outside of you is additionally inside you. You can never be independent from your own wellspring of excellence.

With melancholy we will in general sink into ourselves, stopping the light inside us, and closing out the light of our general surroundings. We feel detached and dis-locked in. Taking yourself on a delight walk is an approach to reconnect to the wealth of life and reconnect on the planet. Simply seeing the stirring of the leaves in the tree and considering how brilliant that sound is, as though the tree is addressing you, or watching a flying creature fly over head, with quality and speed as it takes off in the sky, that feathered creature is alive and moving with reason, take that vitality within yourself, as though you are drinking up the experience and make it your own. Like the flying creature, you can move with quality and reason. The lovely blue of the sky, the light of the moon, the dynamic shades of blossoms, these are all piece of nature's significant excellence and flawlessness of life, similarly as you seem to be, similarly as each individual may be. Take in the significant excellence of nature and liken yourself to it, blend with it, become it and permit it to become you as well. This excellence is within.

Probably the best revelation of my life, and potentially the best thing I accomplish for my self, my body, brain and soul is to take my 'Magnificence Walks'. The Native American Indian's have an articulation hat I have adored since the day I previously found it, I saw it on a guard sticker once and I have been searching for that guard sticker from that point onward. It said "Stroll in Beauty". How superb is that?

I have been a walker for a long time, it is my preferred type of activity, it is the manner in which I contemplate and plan my innovative undertakings. It is the way I de-stress and discharge the trash that scrounges through my psyche. Strolling is an extraordinary method to ground yourself and course vitality. It is cadenced and it is the least demanding most regular type of activity. I have experience with regular wellbeing and mending, I have contemplated and polished the recuperating crafts of shading, sound, contact, fragrance based treatment, nourishment and vitality treatments for a considerable length of time.

I comprehend that a sound psyche, body and soul lead to a more noteworthy feeling of euphoria, prosperity and harmony for the duration of our lives and I utilize the devices of these different recuperating modalities to implant my own life just as those of my customers. I have likewise realized that "magnificence is entirely subjective", an articulation we as a whole learn as youngsters. To see excellence is to be magnificence, this is something we have all heard however how regularly do we recall it?

I don't have a clue when it happened precisely, it was a slow procedure however eventually, I understood I was consolidating every one of these parts together and transformed my day by day strolls into what I call 'Excellence Walks'. I am glad to state it; I really tell individuals I am going on my Beauty Walk, as hokey as it might sound, since I realize it is a roused activity. I have imparted this enlivened activity to numerous young ladies, ladies and men planning to rouse them as well, offering them an instrument to feel more wellbeing and completeness in their day by day lives. I share it since I am motivated each time I go for my magnificence stroll and the key component to the entire procedure is imbuing my self with excellence, it is an absolutely arousing experience. I will include that I trust I am turning out to be increasingly more wonderful as a lady and an individual all around in view of these strolls.

As far as I can tell of the Beauty Walk, I will concede that the initial ten minutes or so are tied in with decompressing. All the stuff of the day whirls through my head, my issues and disillusionments, assignments I have to complete, things I am awkward about and so on. Every last bit of it surfaces until I get into the cadence and begin seeing what is around me.

At the point when you genuinely go for your Beauty Stroll, I welcome you to see the magnificence, even in a city, inside everything around you any place you might be.

Notice design, shades of homes and structures, check whether you can discover the excellence in an individual strolling by you. Open yourself to being a reflection of excellence and be the magnificence that you see. You can utilize this to move your own type of activity or use it as a contemplation to ground, focus and decorate yourself at wheneve

Looking delightful is something imperative for most ladies on the planet since it is viewed as a significant thought to make more men intrigued by them. For this situation, it is prompted for you to know some beneficial things that can make you to glance progressively delightful positively. Additionally, those things will assist you with being progressively wonderful normally so you can make yourself look extraordinary for the vast majority. This article will give you more data about those things so you will recognize what you should do.

Skin
You have to keep the dampness of your skin so you can show the excellence of your skin. For your body skin, you can utilize the results of normal oils which are appropriate with the kind of your skin. For your face skin, you have to wash your face regular so you can keep the neatness of your skin and you should utilize the correct item for your requirements. Discussing excellence items, you should be certain that they are ok for your skin so you can forestall the awful thing that can happen, for example, skin inflammation. For those items, you are encouraged to pick the regular ones that are produced using common fixings. Despite the fact that they are expensive, the outcomes gave are likewise extraordinary.
Hair
Hair is likewise something else you should mind fro on the off chance that you might want to be normally excellent. You have to wash your hair other than the utilization of hair cream. For this situation, it is better in the event that you pick natural cleanser since it gives the best advantages for your eyes.

The utilization of loads of water can likewise assist you with keeping the glossy of your hair so you should drink it more. In addition, the utilization of sound nourishments is likewise a basic interesting point.

Certainty feeling

Other than caring yourself, you have to show your certainty. An inclination that has an extraordinary effect on your life. This sort of feeling is extremely significant on the off chance that you might want to show your lovely side. You should realize that your excellence isn't just about physical appearance yet additionally about your conduct. On the off chance that you have certainty feeling, you will have the option to improve your psychological state so you can confront anything in your life. You should realize that this inclination will lead you to be certain so you can improve in confronting any sort of condition in your life

In this day and age of industrialism and large scale manufacturing, it is smarter to affirm your uniqueness by adhering to the characteristic magnificence rehearses that have been given to you. You needn't bother with items that have synthetic substances in them or items that have been tried on creatures so as to cause you look or to feel lovely.

The really delightful ladies and men are the ones who are acceptable and solid within and simply mirror that in their outward appearance. The best and everlasting methods of magnificence are normal and very straightforward.

The first and most basic excellence tip is this: drink in any event eight glasses of water a day. Convey a jug or two with your any place you proceed to take tastes at visit interims. Water is the most beneficial refreshment and washes down the assemblage of undesirable poisons. Water helps smooth and quick processing. At the point when the interior organs are rinsed, it influences the strength of the skin in a positive manner. In the blink of an eye by any means, your skin will look and feel more clear. Imperfections will before long vanish and your composition will level out. Your face will before long sparkle from inside.

Another significant hint! Try not to wear cosmetics! Why subject our skin to unsafe synthetic substances that won't just obstruct your skin yet will cause you to feel grimy. It is more secure and kinder to the skin when you don't wear any cosmetics whatsoever. Take great consideration of the skin, it's the biggest organ you have!

Have early evenings. Build up a sound rest design and rest early. Resting at 10 PM and awakening at 6 PM gives the ideal measure of rest that your body needs, and will bring about you having shining eyes and clear skin.

Wearing hues that suit your skin tone will improve your general appearance definitely. You don't must have the most costly garments, yet conveniently squeezed and clean garments will consistently emit a decent impression in any circumstance. You will look set up and prepared for anything.

Last however not the least-work out! Strolling the pooch or accomplishing progressively exhausting activity animates the body's digestion. This will thus make a progressively energetic appearance and body shape. Cardio practices or routinely visiting the rec center will condition your muscles and give you vitality. Exercise discharges endorphins which thus fulfill you Each lady needs delicate and delightful skin, however a considerable lot of them make some troublesome memories getting what they need. The possibility of lovely regular skin might possibly be engaging you, however as time has passed by, we have discovered that normally happening fixings are better for the skin's wellbeing and its appearance. Along these lines, if every characteristic ha not spoke to you before, pause for a minute to think about it.

Nature is about physical appearance, excellence of common things which is encircled by us all over the place. Nature backdrops are something identified with nature itself which speaks to the magnificent enchanting magnificence of nature. Everything identified with nature i.e.wallpapers, topics, screen savers and pictures are very requesting among all. These days everybody needs that their PC screen and their cell phones must appear to be unique from others, they should glance alluring in each viewpoint. One can without much of a stretch change their topics, pictures and backdrops just by downloading them through Internet. There are different connections one can snap to get them all in a couple of moments seconds.

Presently a days there are sufficient number of sites that are offering boundless free downloading of nature pictures for their purchasers. These Nature pictures have an incredible wide range of backdrops and a wide range as indicated by the need which suits ones brain.

We can without much of a stretch get backdrops of sea shores, cloud, open country, lakes, waterways and a lot more by the snap of mouse. We can likewise choose backdrops like butterflies, plants and creatures. We can discover any kind of backdrops as indicated by our own advantage. Consequently, backdrops identified with nature are extremely regular among youth. We can discover it through nature photograph display and of no expense.

The brilliant regular pictures are extremely near our heart. One can pick numerous of nature backdrops and nature photographs through different sites at no expense and change them as per the need. Likewise we can send it to every one of our companions and family members and make it save money on our PC and mobiles screen. Aside from this, nature pictures are likewise extremely normal. Everybody enjoys the photos of regular things as they speak to what is acceptable and lovely on this planet. These look appealing and furthermore cause us to feel quiet and better. It can likewise change our good judgment and cause us to feel the magnificence of nature with no pressure and changes our perspective